Curly Girl Adventures

Top Knot

L. B. Anne

JOA PRESS
FLORIDA

L. B. ANNE

ISBN: 9798544940289

DEDICATION

For the Amazing Girls Scout Troops that contributed to this story. Troop 1045 created the character, Lily. Troop 1383 chose the cover color and created the character, Grace. Troop 1418 created the character, Daisy. Thank you all so much!

Table of Contents

Hooray for Friday

My name is Zuri. I don't like names that start with a Z, but I like mine because it means good, nice, pretty, lovely, and cute. All of that is definitely me.

I am seven years old now. That means I can stay up as late as I want, and I can drink coffee. Do not tell my mom. She doesn't know about either of those things.

"IT'S FRIDAY!" I screamed when I awoke this morning. My dad ran down the hall to my room, thinking something was wrong with me, and hit his toe on the dresser. He hopped around on one foot with only his right eye open.

"Good morning, Daddy!" I shouted, stood on my bed, and leapt at him.

WOOSH!

He caught me and laughed. "Zuri, you can't jump at someone without telling them. What if I missed and didn't catch you?"

"You always catch me. Do you want me to make you breakfast?" I asked.

"How about I make *you* breakfast?"

"Okay."

"You do this every Friday, Zuri."

"That's because I'm excited for the weekend. There won't be any school for two whole days after today." I smiled to myself. Two days without sitting next to Beetle-faced Josh. He's like a booger in my nose. I shouldn't have picked at it, I can't shake it off my finger, and it's annoying and gross!

On Saturdays, I didn't have to wake up early, rush to eat breakfast, and catch the school bus. We usually had pizza, and I could spend the entire day outside or with Pickle if I wanted, as long as I'd done my chores.

Pickle is my very best friend, but she doesn't go to my school. Her real name is Pia. We call her Pickle because she would eat pickles for breakfast, lunch, and dinner if her dad didn't make her eat real food. And I don't mean the sweet kind of pickle. She will make a barf face if you give her the sweet kind.

Pickle is homeschooled and has curly hair like mine. We created a club called the Curly Girls Club. We love natural hair and raise our fists in the air and shout, "PROUD TO BE CURLY!"

Anyway, I was saying I had to get my chores done before I could go to Pickle's house. One time, I tried to hurry and push everything under my bed, so my floor looked spick and span, but my mom found it. So now when I yell, "Mommy, my room is clean, can I go now?" she says, "Even under your bed?"

Listen, people, you can't get anything past moms, so do not even try. That's what I've learned in all my seven years. My mom knew it was me who took Lauren's cat from next door and hid him in the clothes hamper. She knew it was me who made the pot of brussel sprouts disappear so we wouldn't have to eat them. (My dad high-fived me for that one.) And somehow, she always knows I'm the one who leaves something open like the refrigerator, the front door, and the peanut butter jar.

On Saturdays, I didn't have to deal with that woman either. My older sister, Lela. She makes my nerves shake. But on Saturdays she's usually Lela-nice so she can go to soccer practice instead of getting grounded.

Lela-nice means she may boss me around, but it's not too bad. She doesn't do anything to make me snap. And everyone knows what happens when I snap. Remember? Geckos in her bed. Gluing the tops of her nail polish to the bottles.

Putting an earthworm on the plate with her spaghetti. She almost ate it. I got grounded forever for that one.

Today, I ran home from the school bus quick in a hurry. Noah and Kai ate my dust. I heard that in a movie, and I've been saying it ever since.

"Zuri, Pickle is calling you!" my mom said as I came in through the garage door.

"She is? Thanks, Mommy."

She handed me the phone.

"Hey, Pickle! I'm coming over," I told her. Then I glanced up at my mom to make sure it was okay. She nodded and walked into the family room. I followed with the phone to my ear, hearing the beat of a song I liked.

Boom-Ba-Boom-Boom it went and I shook my hips.

"Auntie Blithe, what are you watching?"

"Hey, Zuri baby. This is a video of my old double Dutch tournament from when I was a little older than you."

"I'll call you back, Pickle. Yes, Auntie Blithe is here. You should come to my house this time. Bye."

Auntie Blithe sat on the sofa. I hugged her and sat on the floor beside her. "That's in New York, right?"

"Yes, ma'am. It sure is."

Teams of girls jumped rope in a gym much larger than the one at my school. The stands on

one side were full of teams wearing the same colored shirts. On the other side of the gym, people sat cheering the jumpers on.

The girls on the gym floor held two ropes, turning them in opposite directions. Then one or two girls jumped into the center and spun around, doing different tricks as they jumped. One turned a flip.

"Oh, wow. I bet I could do that."

"No, you couldn't," said Lela, sitting on the arm of the sofa. "It looks easy, but it isn't. You're too small anyway."

"I bet I could. Don't you think so, Auntie?"

"You sure could, Baby Girl. Look, that's me. I was ten years old," said Auntie Blithe.

Auntie Blithe's team wore red shorts, white t-shirts, and the same black sneakers. Her hair was in a thick ponytail, and the girl who jumped in the ropes with her had a long French braid. They hopped on one foot, then crossed their feet, and turned around as they jumped.

"Who are the people with the clipboards wearing the white pants and tops?" I asked.

"Those are the judges," said Auntie Blithe.

"Hey, that's a boy."

"Yep, boys can jump too."

A male voice announced, "Jumpers are ready." A horn sounded and a girl jumped in, leaned forward, and looked as if she were running in place superfast.

"What's she doing?"

"That's called speed pairs. Another girl will jump in after her time is up."

I stood and hopped from left to right as if the floor was too hot to step on.

Auntie Blithe laughed. "That's not quite it, but you have potential."

"Will you teach me?"

"Have you got ropes?"

"I sure do."

"Well, then? What are you waiting for? Let's do it."

I stuck my tongue out at Lela.

"This is going to be a disaster," she mumbled, following us.

Zuri's First Double Dutch

We were outside in front of the house when Pickle rolled into the driveway on her electric wheelchair. "Hey, Gram!" I yelled.

"Hello, Zuri. What have you guys got going on over here?" she asked, watching Auntie Blithe and Lela turn the ropes. My grandmother lives with Pickle and her dad. Pickle's father and my father are brothers.

Auntie Blithe stopped, hugged Gram, and turned to Pickle. "Pia, look at you with your cute self!" She kissed her on the cheek. "Are you doing okay?"

"Yes, ma'am," said Pickle with a grin. Everyone loved Auntie Blithe. You were nuts if you didn't. She was fun, kind, had the best jewelry, clothes, and hair. And she liked Pixar movies, just like me.

Auntie Blithe also called me every week just to talk about what was going on at school, like how I put Josh in a headlock or about how the Curly Girls Club was going or whatever else I wanted to talk about.

"Hey, Pickle Eater," Lela said before kissing Gram on the cheek.

Pickle giggled.

Auntie Blithe held the ropes out to Gram. "We need someone else to turn so I can show Zuri how to jump in. Do you want to give it a try?"

"No, I'm going to get inside, out of this heat," Gram replied while waving a folding hand fan at her face.

I looked around our cul-de-sac and up the street for another turner. Kai or Lauren could help, but they weren't outside.

"Pickle?"

"No, I don't think so. But I would try if I had my wrist braces on."

Pickle has brittle bone disease. The scientific name for it is Osteogenesis Imperfecta. It took me forever to learn to pronounce that. You can just call it OI. It means her bones break easily, and that's really painful. That's why she has to be careful with everything she does.

"Oh, I know," said Auntie Blithe. "Lela, you help Zuri, so we can show her how to turn the ropes."

"I don't need her help," I said while snatching the ropes from Lela.

Lela snatched them back. "Yes, you do."

We pulled back and forth on the ropes like we were having a tug of war battle. Lela almost dragged me across the driveway.

"Stop it, you two. Zuri, let her help you," said Auntie Blithe.

"Fine," I mumbled, walking to the sidewalk. Pickle backed up, and Lela stood behind me with her hands over mine. She tried to turn my hands, but I held them as stiff as a board.

"Zuri, stop being difficult," she said.

Auntie Blithe placed her hands on her hips and frowned. "Ladies, if you're going to fight, I'll just go back inside. There's a lot of other things I could be doing, but you asked me to teach you."

I didn't want my aunt to be upset with me, so I relaxed my arms and Lela turned them. The ropes made big loops and tapped the ground slightly as they came down.

"Good," said Auntie Blithe, turning the other end.

"You've got it, Curly Girl!" Pickle exclaimed, cheering me on. That's what besties do.

"I've got it now, Lela."

"Suit yourself," she said, letting go of my hands and backing away.

I tucked in my lips and got ready to show them how fast I learned. I lifted the ropes, making circles with my arms, but my loops looked nothing like when Lela helped me.

My left arm spread out to the left and my right arm stayed low in front of me. I couldn't get the ropes to act right. There was one big loop and one little one. Who could jump in that? The ropes would smack them in the head.

"You're Zuri the Great," Pickle whispered. She always reminded me of my superhero name when I was sad. But I didn't feel so great. I stopped turning the ropes, disappointed in myself. I felt like I did when my dad took my training wheels off my bike and I jumped right on, thinking I could ride. I couldn't. I wobbled and fell in front of everyone.

"You just need practice," said Auntie Blithe.

A car pulled into the next driveway beside our house. Lauren got out of the back seat. "Hey, Zuri! Can we play too?"

A girl, wearing a vest with various kinds of badges on it, walked around the car.

"This is Lily," said Lauren.

"Hi. This is my aunt and my cousin, Pia."

Lela cleared her throat.

"That's my pet—"

"Zuri!"

"I mean, my sister, Lela." I was really going to say my pet goat.

Lauren noticed me checking out Lily's vest. "Oh, she's a girl scout."

"Oh."

Lily's hair was in a big messy bun, and she was munching on a handful of popcorn. "I know how to turn," she said as stuffed her mouth and brushed her hands off on her jeans.

"You do?" asked Lauren, surprised.

"Let's give it a try," said Auntie Blithe.

Lily took the ropes. "I'm a good turner. I don't get to at home because I'm the only girl. I have two older brothers. They play with each other and tease me all the time. But my troop are my sisters. That's part of the Girl Scout Law. We recite it every meeting. My mom is a co-leader."

"Does she always talk so much?" I whispered to Lauren.

She nodded.

"We should start a Curly Girl Scouts," I told Pickle.

She shook her head at me.

Lela turned one end, and Lily turned from the other. She made large circles with her arms.

"That's it! You've got it," said Auntie Blithe.

"Told ya," said Lily.

I frowned at that girl. Why couldn't my turns look like that?

Auntie Blithe rocked forward and back before jumping inside the ropes. She leaned down some because of her height, laughing the whole time.

Her feet went *tappity tap, tappity tap*.

"I feel like a kid again," she said and jumped out of the ropes without them having to stop. She was good.

After seeing how much fun she had, I was excited. "My turn!"

"Go ahead, give it a try," said Auntie Blithe.

I rocked back and forth outside of the ropes as they turned. It was the same thing I saw her do, but I didn't stop rocking. I couldn't figure out when to run into the ropes without hitting them.

"Watch the outside rope," said Auntie Blithe. "When it goes up, jump in."

I watched it, but it didn't work.

"Now!" Pickle exclaimed.

WOMP!

I ran right into the ropes.

"Let's try this," said Auntie Blithe. She stood me in the center of the two ropes.

"This isn't how you did it."

"No, but it is how you learn. Everyone starts double Dutch this way."

I blew air hard out of my nose and looked down at the sidewalk with my hands at my sides until Auntie Blithe told me to jump.

I tried five times, but my feet kept hitting the ropes. Lela was right. I would never be able to jump double Dutch.

"Don't worry, you'll get it," said Auntie Blithe. "If you really want to learn and be good at it, don't give up. Keep trying."

I believed her, so that's what I did. Every day after school, we practiced. Neli (another Curly Girl Club member), Lily, Lauren, and Kai tried to help me get better while Pickle yelled, "You can do it, Curly Girl!"

I think my mom was happy that I wasn't thinking about hair stuff for a while. She didn't have to worry about me trying to create a new hair product.

Then, one day I rocked back and forth, ready to jump in, but I couldn't. I just knew I would hit the ropes.

Noah darted across the street with Omari and hid behind a tree. Why were boys so weird? No one was even chasing them. I ignored them and focused. Lauren and Lily turned the ropes.

"Get ready, Zuri. You're going to do it this time," Lauren said.

"I'm going to give you a box of Girl Scout cookies if you do," said Lily.

Instead of closing my eyes and running in like I usually did, I watched for the rope closest to me to go up. Suddenly something exploded behind me, and I jumped inside the ropes.

"You're doing it!" yelled Pickle.

"Keep jumping!" Lela exclaimed from the front door. And I did.

My friends cheered when I stopped, and even Lela ran over, happy for me.

"Now we know how to get you in there," said Pickle.

"How?"

"Noah has to set off firecrackers behind you."

New Hair Product

I jumped double Dutch!

I was proud of myself and in a good mood the rest of the day.

After dinner, I leaned against Lela's doorway and watched her. That was as far as she allowed me in without permission.

"Whatcha doing, Lela?" I sang.

"Shouldn't you be outside playing with your little friends before it gets dark out?"

"I don't have little friends. Seventh grade doesn't make you an adult, you know?"

"It makes me old enough to do my own hair."

"So what? What are you doing to it anyway?" I asked as I grabbed her door handle, pushing and pulling on the door so that the hinges squeaked.

"Stop doing that. You watch me do my hair all the time. You know what I'm doing." Lela picked up a spray bottle and sprayed around her hairline.

"No, I don't."

"Yes, you do. Stop lying. What do you think I'm doing?"

"Being a brat?"

Her face snarled at me in the mirror.

"Okay, are you gelling your edges?" I asked.

"I told you, you knew."

"So they'll be smooth, right?"

Lela didn't respond as she pulled her hair up high and placed a hair tie around it.

"Well?"

"If you're going to wear a top knot, you need to gel your edges." She looked at my hair. "And not have all of those flyaways like you do."

"There's nothing wrong with my hair." I looked at my reflection in her mirror. My ponytail was low, not high like Lela's, and it spread out every which way. Then I noticed how neat hers looked.

Do not go in, I told my feet, but they didn't listen and slowly stepped into Lela's room. There was a black jar on her dresser. I picked it up. The writing was too tiny on the back. "What's in this stuff anyway?"

"You're in my room."

"Answer the question, Woman. Then I'll leave."

She snatched the jar from me, so I sat on her bed. "I *said,* what's in it?"

"Get off my bed."

"Not until you tell me. Stop being difficult."

"Mommy!" Lela yelled.

"Okay, okay," I said and hopped off. "I don't need you to tell me. I'm going to look it up on your laptop." I snatched it off her bed and ran into the hall. She chased me and leaned over me like a bear, reaching for it.

"You're going to ruin your hair," I told her.

"Give it back!"

"Zuri and Lela!"

We froze and then stood up as straight as soldiers. I handed the laptop to Lela.

"What's going on?" asked our mom.

"Nothing. We were playing. I'm just waiting for Lela to tell me about her hair."

She looked at Lela, who nodded and pulled me toward her room. "Yes, she's telling the truth. Heh, we'll be going now."

Our mom watched us, and Lela closed her bedroom door.

"You're always getting us in trouble," she whispered.

"Just tell me what's in it. I've got things to do."

She frowned at me. "There are a lot of different types of hair gel. But this one contains gelatin and water, and aloe and—Wait a minute. What am I doing?"

I grinned at her.

"Don't you even think about it, Zuri."

"Think about what? Thanks, Lela," I said as I walked away.

"I saw that smirk. You better not try to make any, Zuri. I'm serious. You couldn't anyway. You know what happens every time you try to make stuff."

Why did she have to tell me I couldn't make my own gel? I had no choice now but to try.

...

"Pickle," I said, watching her on my tablet. She must have just washed her hair because it was dripping on a towel that draped over her shoulders. "Does my hair look wild to you?"

"It looks like it normally does."

"But is it wild?" I asked as I rubbed my hand over the front. "Like I need it to lay down?"

"Your hair is curly. Curly hair sticks up."

"But it's supposed to lay flat when it's in a ponytail, isn't it?"

"Look at mine, what do you think?" said Pickle, turning her head side to side.

"Yours doesn't count. You just washed it. I think we need gel for our edges."

"We used to use spit, remember?"

"Gross. We're almost ad-dol-es—"

"Adolescents," Pickle said with ease. "But we were babies."

"Yes, so we don't wash our faces or lay down our edges with saliva like we did when we were—how old were we—three?"

"Five."

We both laughed hysterically. "No, we weren't. I have—"

Pickle cut me off. "A big idea, right?"

"You said it, Pickle. We are going to make our own hair gel so we can have the best top knots ever."

"But I don't want a top knot."

"That's because you haven't used gel. What do you think?"

"As long as we do not get in trouble, I'm in. That means we need permission."

The P-word. Everyone always threw that word around whenever I tried to do anything.

· · ·

My cell phone buzzed as soon as I finished talking with Pickle. "Hello?"

"Zuri, it's me, Auntie Blithe."

"Hey, Auntie."

"Guess what? There is a double Dutch tournament coming to Orlando, and if you want to, you can put a team together to compete."

"Really? I can?" I was so excited I flipped over the back of the sofa and dropped the phone.

I ran into the kitchen. "Mommy, can I? Auntie Blithe already talked to you, right? Did she tell you?"

I could hear Auntie Blithe yelling my name through the phone. "Zuri!"

"I don't know, Zuri. You're always getting involved with something," my mom said as she took the phone from me and talked to Auntie Blithe.

I held onto her arm. "Please, please, please. I won't ask for anything ever again. I'll keep my room clean, and I won't get into any trouble. I promise," I said, holding up my hand like I was swearing to tell the truth like in court. My other hand was behind my back with my fingers crossed.

"Okay," she said, and I jumped up and down and put my arms around her waist, squeezing as hard as I could.

I knew just who I would have on my team. My Curly Girls Club, Lauren, and Lily. And I could not wait to tell them.

...

In class the next day, I worked on my team list at my desk. Then I felt air blowing at my ear. Josh was being a snoop and breathing over my shoulder, trying to read my paper. I slammed my hands flat on top of my paper, covering it.

"Stop it, Josh. Go and sit down."

"I saw my name. You wrote something about me."

"I did not." He was the last person I would add to my team.

That nosey girl, Jamie, looked around for Mr. Bugsby and then pointed at us.

My friend, Zoey, jumped out of her seat and ran over.

"Zoey, get back to your desk," Mr. Bugsby said.

"Stop it, Josh," Zoey whispered. "Proud to be curly," she told me with her fist in the air. Sometimes I wondered if I should have made her a member of the Curly Girls Club. Zoey didn't know when to be proud to be curly.

"Are you two not getting along again?" asked Mr. Bugsby.

Josh hurried and sat at his desk. "We're good. Go back to what you were doing. Teach us something."

Mr. Bugsby's forehead wrinkled as he brought his lips together into thin lines. Then he turned back to his dry erase board that took up almost the whole wall.

As soon as Mr. Bugsby looked away, Josh tiptoed away from his desk.

"Oh, Mr. Bugsby!" I sang and pointed.

"Josh, get back to your seat."

"I don't like math."

"That doesn't explain why you are out of your seat."

"I need my special eraser." He walked to his cubby and grabbed something out of his backpack.

Mr. Bugsby turned away to finish teaching the lesson. I watched Josh place his rectangle-shaped eraser on his desk. It wasn't pink like I had expected.

"That doesn't look like any eraser I've seen."

He took the wrapper off.

"Hey, that's gum."

Josh grinned and chewed like a chipmunk. He didn't even offer me half. What a waste. He was about to get in trouble and throw out a perfectly good piece of gum that he could have eaten after school.

I raised my hand as I watched him. But before Mr. Bugsby could notice me, the boy on the other side of Josh said, "Mr. Bugsby, Josh has gum."

He took my rights away. I was the one he annoyed all the time. I wanted to tell on him.

"No, I don't," said Josh.

That beetle-faced boy tried to swallow it and started to choke.

I stood and raised my hand to hit him on the back, but Mr. Bugsby caught my arm.

"That won't do," he said. He knelt beside Josh and placed a hand on his chest with his other on his back. "Cough, Josh, keep coughing."

Josh turned pink, and soon we were all yelling, "Cough, Josh!" and coughing along with him. Then Mr. Bugsby leaned him forward and whacked him five times on the back.

"Eww," someone said when the pink glob of gum dropped from Josh's mouth.

Mr. Bugsby saved the beetle.

Zuri's Team

"PROUD TO BE CURLY!" Neli said when she saw me in gym class. There were three classes all in the same gym period.

"Proud to be curly," I responded. "That's a pretty scarf you have around Susan." All the curly girls had names for our hair. I call my hair Shelby.

"I know! Tie dye is my new favorite." She knelt to tie her shoelaces.

"I heard Josh almost died in class today. Did he really eat poison?"

"Who told you that? People are always making up stories. He choked on gum."

"Oh. I bet that was scary for him."

"Him? I almost had a heart attack."

I looked at the other side of the gym. My eyes bulged from my head as I pulled Neli toward me. "Neli, look at that girl. Who is that?"

The girl did three somersaults in a row.

"Oh, that's Daisy. She's into gymnastics. Ballet too."

"Do you think she could do a flip like that while jumping rope?"

"You mean for the double Dutch competition? Let's ask her."

We ran across the gym, but Crazy Grace blocked us off. She pushed her glasses up over her nose and glared at us.

Crazy Grace wasn't in my class, but everyone knew her because she could be a bully sometimes. She loved pink and wore it almost every day. Pink shoes, pink shirt, pink pants, pink headband over her long brown hair.

"Where are you two trying to go? Get back over there before I report you," said Grace.

"Report us?" That girl made me mad. I twisted my face into a growl, but I didn't shake my body at her. I was a year older. I couldn't do that baby stuff anymore.

"Mrs. Peet, they're on the wrong side of the gym," said Grace.

Mrs. Peet wore black joggers and a purple hoodie with a whistle hanging from her neck. She walked over to us.

"That's why your earring is about to fall out," I told Grace.

She grabbed her ear.

"Grace, I've told you before that you can't wear dangling earrings in gym," Mrs. Peet said. "Take them off. I'll hold them for you until class is over."

Grace shot us a mean look.

I rolled my eyes. "What? We didn't tell you to wear them."

She stood there, watching us walk over to Daisy.

"This is Zuri," said Neli.

"Oh, the Curly Girl, right?" Daisy said. She lifted her leg behind her, bent her knee, and grasped her ankle.

She'd heard of me. That Daisy made me smile. "You're good at gymnastics stuff."

"Yep. I take lessons."

"Have you ever jumped double Dutch?"

"Nope."

"Rope?"

"Have I jumped rope? Of course."

"Can you turn a flip while you jump rope?"

"I can do summersaults, backflips—anything."

Neli and I looked at each other with bright eyes. "Do you want to be on my team?"

"A Curly Girl? I mean I *am* curly too."

"Uh, I meant on my double Dutch team."

"Oh. Double Dutch? What's that?"

I threw my hands in the air. "Doesn't anyone know about double Dutch? What's wrong with everyone?"

Daisy looked confused at me as I huffed.

"Don't worry about her," Neli whispered to Daisy, even though I could hear her. "She gets like this sometimes. We ignore it."

...

During our ride home on the school bus, I invited Omari to my house. He and Pickle arrived at the same time, and we told him about double Dutch.

"I am not jumping rope with girls," he said.

I put my hands on my hips.

"Don't upset him," Pickle whispered. "You've jumped rope with us before, Omari."

"This is different."

"It's double Dutch," I said.

"In front of everyone? Nope."

"You can do it. It's your right under the constitution."

"You don't even know what that is."

"Yes, I do," I said and began singing, "We the people..."

Lela shook her head. "That's just the introduction to the constitution."

I sang louder.

Omari covered his ears, and I chased him around the front yard singing.

"Leave him alone already," said Lela. "If he does not want to do it, he doesn't have to. Sheesh, you're not his boss."

I ignored her. "Get in the house, Omari."

"Huh?"

"I want to show you something."

"Noah, Hector," I called to them from across the street and waved them over to my house.

I showed them Auntie Blithe's videotape. They didn't even know what a videotape was.

"See, that's a boy right there. Look how good he is. It's a competition. He's the best one. That could be you," I said.

"What do we have to do?" asked Noah.

"No hair products, right?" asked Omari.

Hector laughed. "Oh yeah, that pickled pudding stuff. That was funny."

I rolled my eyes at him. "No hair stuff. Scout's honor."

"You're not a scout."

"Yet."

Noah waved Omari and Hector in closer, and they whispered to each other. A couple of seconds later, they turned to me. "We're in."

"You can't just be in. You have to try out for a spot on the team."

"Now she tells us," said Omari.

...

We were back outside when Kai ran up to us laughing, her sister, Kimmie, following behind her.

I gasped. "Kai, look at your sister."

Kai turned and laughed even harder.

Kimmie wore a light blue princess costume and, instead of her usual toy crown, she wore a pair of her underwear on her head with a ponytail sticking through each hole where her legs should go.

"She thinks it's a hat," said Kai. "She'll scream if you try to take it off her."

And I thought *I* played jokes on people. This was much worse. "Kai..."

"Okay, okay. Take it off, Kimmie."

"No," she screamed and covered her head with her arms.

"Kimmie, are you making a green decision? You want to make green choices, don't you?" asked Kai.

"Green?" Pickle asked.

"That's what they do at her preschool, so we do it at home too. A green decision or reaction is a good one."

"Don't you want to make a green decision, Kimmie?" I asked.

"Green," Kimmie said, letting Kai take the underwear off her head.

"You should be nicer to her," I told Kai.

"Are you nice to your sister?" she asked.

"I sure am."

Kai pursed her lips at me.

"I mean if I had a little sister, I'd be nice to her. I'm the little sister, and that woman is not nice to me."

"See. And why do you call Lela 'that woman?' It's so weird." She laughed.

Lela glanced over but didn't say anything. She sat on the porch step watching us practice every day.

"We're going to have to give Kimmie something to do," I said.

"Let her count and then we'll jump in," Kai suggested. "You got it, Kimmie?"

She nodded. "Tree, two, one!" She couldn't say three.

"She's counting backward," said Noah.

"Does it matter?" I asked.

Omari stood in the middle of the ropes and waited for me and Kai to turn them.

"Tree, two, one!" Kimmie said.

Omari tried to jump.

"Tree, two, one!"

Noah tried.

"Tree, two, one!"

Hector tried.

I rubbed my hands over my face as Lela walked up to me and said, "They're going to need a lot of work."

Grasshoppers

"Mommy, I need you to schedule a Zoom meeting for the Curly Girl Club."

She laughed. "A Zoom meeting? Kids don't do that."

"Yes, they do. It's important. Please?"

"Can't one of the other Curly Girl parents do it?"

"They don't know about it. I'm the president and I'm calling an emergency meeting."

My mom sat at her computer while I stood beside her, waiting to slip into her seat.

"PROUD TO BE CURLY!" each Curly Girl said when she came on.

"What's up, Zuri?" asked Kayla. "We've never done this before."

I looked at the faces of Neli, Pickle, Kayla, and Zoey on the screen. "Tryouts for my double Dutch team have been a disaster. No one knows how to jump. I'm getting better, but it's going to take too long to teach everyone."

"Who's good already? That's what we need," said Pickle.

"That girl, Daisy," said Neli.

"That will be your job, Neli. Talk her into it."

Neli's face filled the screen. "Talk Daisy into it," she said as she wrote it down. "I'm on it. I mean, tomorrow."

"Thanks, Neli."

"There's Lily, the Girl Scout, too," said Pickle.

"I think she'd be in, but no one asked her yet," I said.

"We can get the jump ropes out at recess tomorrow and see who else can jump."

"Good idea, Kayla."

"PROUD TO BE CURLY," Zoey shouted with a fist in the air.

"PROUD TO BE CURLY!" we all responded.

The next day, the Curly Girls practiced double Dutch on the playground during recess. I walked around the field with Zoey, asking girls if they knew how to do it. "What is it?" asked one of them.

I pointed at Kayla.

"That's cool," she said.

"Nope, she's never tried. Moving on," said Zoey, pulling me away. "Zuri, look!"

Beetle-face Josh charged at Neli and Kayla as they turned the ropes.

"He better not! I'm going to get him," I said as I ran.

"Me too," said Zoey. She ran after me.

"Josh!" I screamed.

He ran right to the ropes, jumped in, and then jumped out without hitting the ropes.

I stopped running.

"Did you just see what I saw?" asked Zoey.

"You've got to be kidding me," I said. "Josh, do that again."

He happily ran back a few steps and then forward into the ropes again, this time behind Daisy.

Zoey and I raced over to them.

"Josh, you're—"

"Jumping rope?" His voice vibrated as he jumped.

He finally stopped, landing on top of the ropes. The girls ran up to pat him on the back.

"What's all this for?" he asked, shaking his shoulders to avoid their pats. I knew then that he had just wanted to annoy us. He didn't expect to be praised for charging into our fun.

"Zuri…" said Kayla with a raised eyebrow.

"I know, but I can't. We cannot have him on the team. It will be horrible."

"But he's good."

"Listen, Woman, good is one thing. A nuisance is another."

"I'm going to ask him," said Kayla.

"I can't watch this happen. I'm going inside."

...

Josh agreed to jump with us, but we had to bribe him with Girl Scout cookies and fill his game card from his favorite arcade with twenty-five chips. We all put our money together for that kid. That's how good he was.

Daisy said yes also, as long as it didn't interfere with gymnastics lessons, and then she added, "And can I be a Curly Girl?"

Kayla moved my head up and down to say yes.

We all met Auntie Blithe at the community center. She said we needed to get used to jumping on the gym floor. "We've got the gym for one hour."

First, Auntie Blithe had us all sit on the floor while she explained the rules of double Dutch. Pickle came too.

"There are two types of teams. There's a single team with three members–two turners, one jumper, and a double team with four members–two turners, two jumpers."

Josh stood and pointed around at everyone, counting.

"Josh, sit still. This is important. There are three tests. In the first, jumpers must complete a set of tricks in a certain amount of time; the second is a speed test in which the number of jumps are counted; and the third is a freestyle."

"Like dancing?" I asked.

"Kind of, but you're jumping. You do a trick routine of whatever you want to do."

Josh raised his hand. "That's for me."

"Noted," said Auntie Blithe. Pickle held up a notepad that looked bigger than her and wrote it down.

"Here are the tricks you need to learn for the first round:

1) Two turns to the right, jump on the right foot.

2) Two turns to the left, jump on the left foot.

3) Two crisscross jumps in which the right foot crosses in front of the left.

4) Two crisscross jumps in which the left foot crosses in front of the right.

5) Ten high steps, alternating feet (the jumper must jump ten times on each foot), raising the knee to waist level."

Lela did each trick as Auntie Blithe read them from Pickle's notepad.

"That's easy," said Daisy.

"I can't do all of that," said Omari.

"You don't have to. I'm going to figure out who does what today," said Auntie Blithe.

I leaned back on my elbows and listened.

"The speed round means jumping as fast as you can within two minutes." She showed us how to stand. "Your upper body remains very still."

Then Lela showed us how to run in place fast.

"The freestyle part we talked about earlier is one minute. You cannot go over one minute or go less than forty-five seconds."

"Or what happens?" asked Noah.

"They take points off." She looked at Josh. "In freestyle, you have to do things like turns, acrobatics, dance, and an ending."

"Like in gymnastics," said Daisy.

"That sounds hard," said Noah.

"Told ya," said Omari.

"Zuri, jumpers can't take more than five seconds to enter the ropes."

I sat up. "Okay."

Lily raised her hand. "Will they take off points?"

"Yes, they will. The judges subtract points for mistakes or for dropping a rope. If the jumper has a bad entrance into the ropes or a bad exit jumping out, points may be taken away as well." Auntie Blithe paused to look all of us in the eye. "And this is important. Jumpers are required to maintain their appearance. That means your uniform and hair must be neat. You can't wear any jewelry or hair accessories."

She looked at me when she said that last part.

"You also must have good sportsmanship and positive attitudes."

"That means you can't throw tantrums or yell at anyone," Lela said, looking around Auntie Blithe at me.

"Okay, are we ready?" asked Auntie Blithe.

"We need a name," said Pickle.

"That's right. We do. What do you have in mind? We'll vote on it."

"The Rattlesnakes," yelled Josh.

"Jumping Bunnies," said Lauren.

"Mexican Jumping Beans!" said Hector.

Auntie Blithe laughed.

"Gross. Those have bugs in them. That's why they move," said Kai. "And they're not beans at all."

"How about Grasshoppers," said Auntie Blithe, and looked around at all of us.

All the boys put their hands up in agreement. Then the girls put theirs up too.

"All right, Let's get started."

Auntie Blithe set us up in groups. She played music as we jumped. She said it would help us remember we were also putting on a performance.

I practiced jumping in and out of the ropes. Then I practiced turning.

The Grasshoppers practiced at the gym once a week and at home almost every day. And I couldn't believe I was on a team named after a bug, and that Beetle-faced Josh was on the team too.

Top Knot Trouble

Josh and I were getting along better than ever at school because we were teammates. "We're Grasshoppers," he went around telling everyone. For once, he didn't make my nerves shake, and I wasn't waiting for Friday so I could get away from him.

But Beetle-face messed everything up by saying, "Your hair is too big for double Dutch." Then he stretched his arms out wide as if my hair was that big and acted out how the ropes would bounce off my hair and cause him to tumble over.

"That wouldn't happen."

"Yes, it would. Watch."

I thought about that all day, went home, and stood in the mirror. "My hair needs to be perfect for the competition." I held my hair on top of my head. "It's only one day away."

"You're going to wear a top knot?" Lela asked.

"What's wrong with that?"

"With all the hair you have? Your bun will be huge and hit the ropes. That's a top *not*. Get it? As in do not? Never mind."

"How are you wearing your hair?"

"Just like it is now," said Lela.

"In a top knot?"

"Yeah, but I'm not competing, so it doesn't matter."

My mom walked in and helped me pull my hair into a ponytail. "Maybe we should blow it out some."

"No, that's against Curly Girl rules. But…"

"Yes?"

"Mommy, will you help me make hair gel?"

"We *have* hair gel," said Lela.

"No, I want to make some. Natural."

"Are you actually asking for help?" asked my mom.

"Yes."

"Then I have no choice. You are growing up. Turning seven years old made you more responsible, I think."

I grinned. "Sure did."

"I know just the kind to make. Flaxseed hair gel."

"Flaxseed? Is that good?"

"Yes."

"What else do we need?"

My mom read the recipe from her tablet. "Two cups of water, 1/3 cup of flax seeds, 1/2 teaspoon of 100% honey, and a 1/2 teaspoon of shea butter."

Excited, I hopped around the kitchen. I looked in the magical kitchen drawer that often held whatever we needed and found measuring spoons.

"Pour the water and flax seeds into that pot on the counter." I poured, and only a little water splashed out. "Done!"

My mom stirred it with a wooden spoon. "Can I stir?" I asked.

"No. You and fire are not a good combination. In fact, I don't like how close you are to the stove on that step stool. Back up some."

I climbed down and moved back. The pot began to boil, and my mom removed it from the heat. "We can't let it get too thick.

"Get the big strainer and put it over that bowl so we can separate the seeds from the gel."

"Where's the strainer?" I asked.

"Here," said Lela, handing it to me.

"Okay, now we have to let it cool."

"Are you sure?"

"That's what it says here. For about twenty minutes."

"Twenty minutes is forever. What are we going to do while we wait?"

"I have an idea," my mom said.

She tapped her tablet a few times and a hip hop beat played. She danced around the kitchen island. I laughed and joined her.

Lela watched us from her stool. After a few minutes, I grabbed her hands and pulled her up. I quickly pulled my hands away with eyes wide, remembering she didn't like me touching her. But that woman didn't get mad. She smiled at me and grabbed my hands. We danced with my mom and grabbed her hands too.

The timer buzzed.

"It's time to add the other ingredients," my mom said, out of breath.

I let go of Lela. Dancing with her was fun. It wasn't often that she did stuff like that with me. I was a little sad it was over.

"Zuri, get the honey."

"I'll add the shea butter," said Lela.

"What are we going to store it in?" I asked.

"I have a glass jar," my mom said.

"I want my own jar," said Lela. "A small one."

My mom stirred all the ingredients together. "Now we just need to try it."

"Can I put some on right now?" I asked.

"No. Always try products out on clean hair."

"Then it will lay my edges down?"

"I don't know about that, but it will definitely define your curls."

I looked at Lela. She shrugged and said, "What? I didn't say it would lay it down."

"You said gel is for laying down your edges, not defining curls."

"It's for both."

"All right girls, all you have to do is tie a scarf around your head after you apply it, Zuri."

"Are you sure?"

"Yes. When it cools, we'll do your hair for tomorrow."

"A top knot?"

"If you insist."

That Lela just shook her head and left the room. "She has way too much hair for that," she mumbled.

. . .

I went to bed late and could barely sleep. I was so excited for the tournament, I awoke at 5 AM.

I laid in my unicorn pjs until I couldn't wait anymore. Auntie Blithe brought Grasshopper uniforms for everyone to our last practice. Mine hung neatly over my chair. I lifted the green t-shirt, ran my hand over our team name on the back, and hurried and dressed.

My mom came to my room to check on me and saw that I was up. She unwrapped the scarf from around my hair and fixed my top knot.

"What do you think?" she asked, behind me in the mirror.

"Perfect!" I said and hugged her.

I was downstairs when Lela came pestering me on my big day.

"Zuri, Auntie Blithe said to get a goodnight's sleep, but you barely slept. You don't know how to do stuff quietly. I heard how early you got up. You're going to be so tired today," she said.

"No, I won't," I said as I zipped past her.

"Why not?" she asked.

"I know I just had a full cup of coffee," my mom said from the kitchen.

"What's wrong, Mommy?" asked Lela.

"I must be losing my mind. I poured the creamer in— when did I drink it? There's only half a cup here." I heard her smacking her lips. "I don't even taste it in my mouth."

I shot up from the ground after tying my shoelaces and hopped back and forth. "Are-you-ready-I'm-ready-let's-go-we-don't-want-to-be-late-do-I-need-a-jacket-will-it-be-cold-in-there-where-is-Pickle-can-we-stop-for-donuts-ooo-a-penny-it's-heads up."

"She said all of that in one breath," said Lela.

My mom looked into her coffee cup and back at me. "Zuri!"

...

The Grasshoppers didn't all arrive at the competition together. We would have needed a bus. My family rode in Uncle Frank's van with Pickle and Gram. We arrived at 9 AM. I thought we were early, but there were kids everywhere.

Auntie Blithe stood outside the entrance, talking to a news reporter. She called me over. I felt butterflies in my stomach as I looked into the camera. She put her arm over my shoulders. "This is her first year jumping," she told the news reporter. "She caught on so fast I realized we needed a division for younger jumpers. I reached out to schools and after school clubs in the area to see if anyone would be interested in putting together teams, and I received a great response."

The reporter thanked Auntie Blithe, and we all went inside. There were more teams than I imagined would be there. They were dressed in black bottoms and matching shirts and were already warming up, taking turns hopping in and out of the ropes.

The name of each team was printed on each shirt. There were the Double Sparks, the Leaping Allstars, the Skip Warriors, and more.

I ♡ Double Dutch signs hung from the walls. And even though it was morning, I could smell hot dogs grilling and popcorn popping.

Seeing everyone cheer and clap their hands got me so excited.

"Are we late?" I asked.

"No, but the competition has already started for some," said Auntie Blithe.

"It looks like everyone is older than us."

"Don't worry," Auntie Blithe said. "That's why they added a division for younger jumpers."

Our mouths dropped as we watched one of the teams. A boy jumped by himself, and another boy did the same a few feet away. They jumped toward each other, tossed one end of the rope to the other, and hopped back, turning double Dutch. It was amazing. It was like the ropes were alive and wanted to go into the other person's hand.

"If this is our competition, we're in trouble," said Omari.

"Zuri!"

I turned around. The rest of the Curly Girls Club had arrived—with top knots.

"Zuri, what did you do?" asked Lela.

"What? We look good."

"We sure do," said Zoey.

"Yes, you do, but some of your top knots are too high," said Auntie Blithe.

"Told you," said Lela.

"Especially yours, Zuri. You have a lot of hair. Come over here. We have to bring these down."

"No."

Jumping Time

"I don't think I heard her. Did she say no?" asked Kai.

Pickle's eyes were wide. Lela's mouth dropped. My mom put her hand on her hip. My dad spun around. Gram walked toward me.

"No?" said Auntie Blithe with her brows lifting. "Zuri, remember at practice when I told everyone you must have good sportsmanship and positive attitudes?"

"Yes. But I didn't mean no. I meant do I have to—like is it necessary?"

"If you plan on jumping in this tournament, it is. Do you remember that your appearance is part of the competition? Look at Josh. He got a haircut so he could keep his bangs out of his eyes."

"I don't want to trip on a rope and lose points," Josh said.

I crossed my arms over my chest and frowned.

"She's about to blow," said Neli.

Zoey stood beside me and crossed her arms too. One by one, all the Curly Girls stood together in protest.

"Oh boy, they're taking a stand. It's all for one and one for Curly Girls," said Lela.

"We don't have time for this," said my dad, and I knew he was ready to march me out of there.

Auntie Blithe put her hand up, telling him to wait. "Lela, grab the ropes," she said.

We followed her out into a back hall. Lily arrived and chased us down there. "Your hair is way too big," she said when she saw me.

"That's what they've been trying to tell her," said Kai.

Auntie Blithe had Lily and Lela turn the ropes and told me to jump in. I was ready to show them my top knot was just fine. And just like I thought, it did not hit the ropes. Instead, it flopped all over the place as if it came to life and was trying to escape. "Bobby pins!" I shouted.

"No, you don't need bobby pins. We are lowering everyone's ponytail. Got it?" said Auntie Blithe.

Gram came up the hall. "They need to get out there and warm up. They're up next."

Pickle wheeled her chair next to me. "Hey, Curly Girl," she said, like we hadn't just arrived in the same car.

"Hey, Pickle." My voice sounded like I'd just swallowed nasty cold medicine. The cherry one. My stomach felt like it too.

"I know you're 'proud to be curly' and all, but you can't always have things your way. Look at me. Do you see me being all upset because my bones aren't strong enough to turn the rope for you?"

I'd been staring at black and white specks on the floor but looked up at her. "No."

"I wish I could jump too, but I can't. So I'm happy being Auntie Blithe's assistant so I can still participate."

That Pickle was right, and she always knew what to say to make me calm down. "Lela," I called and pointed at my hair. "Can you help?"

That woman looked shocked.

...

One by one, the teams approached the floor according to grade level. The competition usually started with third graders, but we were the new addition to the tournament.

We stood in front of the judges—four men and four women dressed in white. My knees were shaking. I smiled at them, but they did not smile back. Their faces were blank like statues.

Auntie Blithe watched from the sidelines as we walked onto the gym floor. My heart was about to pound out of my chest.

Once, I heard my dad say something like if anything can go wrong, it's going to happen or something like that. Well, he was right.

First, Lauren was warming up and twisted her ankle. Then Auntie Blithe said, "I know you're all nervous—" But before she could finish, Kai threw up. And Neli was too terrified to leave the sidelines.

"What are we going to do now?" asked Omari.

"I don't know," I said.

"Hold on," said Lily. She pressed her forefinger and thumb together like an OK sign, put them in her mouth, whistled, and waved her hand high in the air.

Some girls ran over. "We're needed, girls," she told them.

"Who are they?"

"They're from my troop. This is what we do. We save the day."

"Can you turn?" asked Auntie Blithe. One girl, Madison, who was a little shy at first, said yes. Another, Alyssa, said she could jump. "Lela, have them switch shirts with Neli and Lauren."

Lela hurried away to the restroom with the girls. They came back quickly.

"Pickle!" Auntie Blithe called.

"Me?" she asked, pointing at herself. She rolled her chair onto the floor.

"You're going to have to turn the ropes."

"I can't," she replied and looked over at Uncle Frank.

"Yes, you can. Don't worry. It will be okay."

I didn't know what Auntie Blithe was doing. She knew Pickle had OI and her bones could break just from moving the wrong way.

She ran over to the judges. They nodded and smiled at Pickle.

Auntie Blithe tied an end of a rope to each handle of Pickle's chair. Lily turned the other end.

"It's working!" she said. Now we had another set of turners.

"Pickle saved the day," I cheered.

First, the single teams went and then the doubles. Lily and I were part of a double team and jumped together. We did high knees, crisscross jumps, and turns. I think I held my breath the whole time.

Omari and Zoey did the speed rounds. I didn't know Zoey's feet could move so fast.

Josh and Daisy jumped freestyle and did cartwheels and flips. They were great. After how horrible we were in practice, somehow it all came together.

Then it was time for us to line up for the judges to announce the winners.

Who Won?

We stood in our neon green shirts and black shorts, all holding hands. I even held Beetle-faced Josh's hand. Only today he wasn't a beetle face. He was Josh, expert flipper.

There were tall trophies on the table and some small ones too. I thought the big one would look good on the mantel in our family room.

"The winner for the second grade division is…" The man paused.

Either my hands were sweaty, or it was Josh's and Lily's.

Why was he waiting so long? "Hurry and say it already," I almost yelled.

"The Jumping Beans!" he exclaimed.

"Hey, that was going to be our name," said Hector.

Josh cried. I think it was him. My eyeballs were sweating, so I couldn't see well.

We started walking away with our heads low.

"Second place goes to… the Grasshoppers."

We kept walking. Auntie Blithe yelled for us to come back. "Did you hear what he said?"

"Did he say us?" I asked.

"You guys came in second place for your division!"

We ran back out, and I hugged Pickle. We did it. We all hopped up and down, cheering for ourselves, and were each given one of the smaller trophies, even Pickle.

Josh got the freestyle champion award for our division. I wanted two trophies like he got.

Lela hugged me. "Zuri, I'm proud of you. I know you think I don't like you. I heard what you said to Kai. But I-I do. We're sisters." With a shove, she added, "Even though you're annoying sometimes."

"We've done it again!" said Lily to her Girl Scout troop. "I wonder if there is a badge for helping win a competition."

"I want a badge!" I told Lily.

"Ask your mom if you can join our troop."

"Okay!"

It was the best day ever. I told you weekends are the best. We all went out to eat at Josh's favorite restaurant, and he got to use his game card he'd bribed us for.

That evening, I watched Lela applying some of the flaxseed gel we made to her hair. "It was a good day, right Lela?"

"Yep."

"We made a good batch of gel too, didn't we?"

"Uh huh."

"We're friends now, right?"

"I guess."

"Then, I have to tell you something, because I feel bad."

She stopped moving. "What?"

"I uh…"

She looked around the room and then sniffed the jar. "What did you do?"

"I'm sorry I put snot in your hair gel!"

"Mommy!"

The End

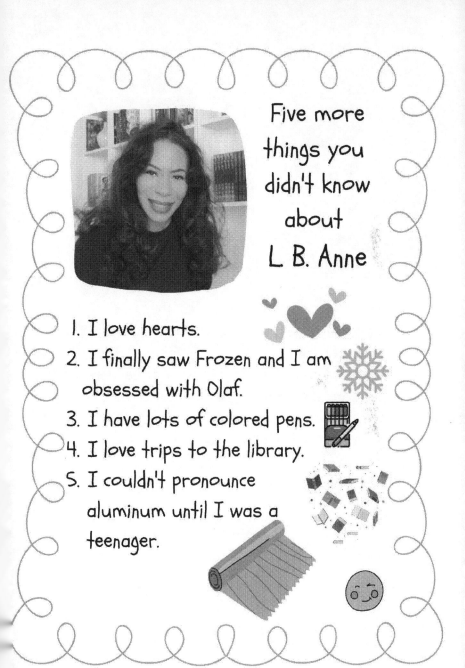

Five more things you didn't know about L B. Anne

1. I love hearts.
2. I finally saw Frozen and I am obsessed with Olaf.
3. I have lots of colored pens.
4. I love trips to the library.
5. I couldn't pronounce aluminum until I was a teenager.

Please Leave a Review

Your review means the world to me. I greatly appreciate any kind words. Even one or two sentences go a long way in helping readers discover the Curly Girl Adventures series.

Thank you in advance.

Books by L. B. Anne

Brave New World, BookOne:
Gemma Kaine Sky Rider

Brave New World, Book, Book Two:
Gemma Kaine The Curse of Mant(a)oming Soon

Lolo and Winkle, Book One:
Go Viral

Lolo and Winkle, Book Two:
Zombie Apocalypse Club

Lolo and Winkle, Book Three:
Frenemies

Lolo and Winkle, Book Four:
Break London

Lolo and Winkle, Book Five:
Middle School Misfit

Lolo and Winkle, The Complete Collection

Sheena Meyer, Book One:
The Girl Who Looked Beyond the Stars

Sheena Meyer, Book Two:
The Girl Who Spoke to the Wind

Sheena Meyer, BookThree:
The Girl Who Captured the Sun

Sheena Meyer, Book Four:
The Girl Who Became a Warrior

Sheena Meyer, Book Five:
City of Gleamers

Everfall, Book One:
Before I let go

Everfall, Book Two
If I Fail

Curly Girl Adventures, Book One:
Pickled Pudding

Curly Girl Adventures, Book Two:
Zuri the Great

Curly Girl Adventures, Book Three:
Tangled

Curly Girl Adventures, BookFour:
Top Knot

Snicker's Wish, Christmas Story

Triskety Spindles Dinosaur Adventures

Five Things About Dragonflies

ABOUT THE AUTHOR

L B. Anne is best known for her Lolo and Winkle book series in which she tells humorous stories of middle-school siblings, Lolo and Winkle, based on her youth, growing up in Queens, New York. She lives on the Gulf Coast of Florida with her husband and is a full-time author and speaker. When she's not inventing new obstacles for her diverse characters to overcome, you can find her reading, playing bass guitar, running on the beach, or downing a mocha iced coffee at a local cafe while dreaming of being your favorite author.

Stay in touch at www.lbanne.com

Facebook: facebook.com/authorlbanne

Instagram: Instagram.com/authorlbanne

Twitter: twitter.com/authorlbanne

Made in the USA
Middletown, DE
14 November 2024